Pout-Pout Fish
Lucky Leprechaun

Written by **Wes Adams**   Illustrated by **Isidre Monés**

Based on the *New York Times*–bestselling Pout-Pout Fish books
written by Deborah Diesen and illustrated by Dan Hanna

Farrar Straus Giroux
New York

Farrar Straus Giroux Books for Young Readers
An imprint of Macmillan Publishing Group, LLC
175 Fifth Avenue, New York, NY 10010

Color separations by Embassy Graphics
Printed in China by RR Donnelley Asia Printing Solutions Ltd., Dongguan City, Guangdong Province
Designed by Aram Kim
First edition, 2019
10 9 8 7 6 5 4 3 2

mackids.com

Library of Congress Control Number: 2018936540
ISBN: 978-0-374-31054-7

Our books may be purchased in bulk for promotional, educational, or business use.
Please contact your local bookseller or the Macmillan Corporate and Premium Sales Department at
(800) 221-7945 ext. 5442 or by e-mail at MacmillanSpecialMarkets@macmillan.com.

Every St. Patrick's Day, Mr. Fish
dresses up in a tall hat and whiskers
and carries a pot of gold.
But this year his pot is empty.

"What a wonderful leprechaun costume!" says Miss Shimmer.
"But my golden treasure is missing," Mr. Fish says. "Leprechauns always carry a pot of gold."

"We'll find it," says his friend. "Wearing green on St. Patrick's Day should bring us all good luck."

Mrs. Squid spreads the word.
"We're looking for the missing treasure," she says.

"Missing treasure?"
echoes Ms. Clam. "Oh my."

Besides his treasure, Mr. Fish has also lost his holiday cheer.
"We must find the missing gold!" declares Mr. Eight.

Up and down, over and under, the creatures follow one another through the sea.

As they parade after the missing treasure, a worried Pout-Pout Fish leads the way.

Underneath the Emerald Isle,
the excited searchers scatter
in every direction.

"If you were golden treasure,
where would you hide?"
Mr. Fish wonders.

"In the big-big dark," says Mr. Lantern.
"Let's see what we can find."

Mr. Lantern and a nervous Mr. Fish swim down, down, down, where they discover a wild array of creatures—but not Mr. Fish's special treasure.

Mr. Fish is glad to leave the depths behind.

"Let's visit my cousins, the Oysters," suggests Ms. Clam. "They know all about hiding treasures."

No luck! Lounging on a sandy bed near the
Sham-Rock, the Oysters explain that they only know
about hiding pearls inside their shells.
Mr. Fish's smile goes further
upside down.

"How about the shipwreck?" says Mr. Eight.

In the hold of a sunken pirate ship, they find a chest of golden coins. "Is this the treasure you are looking for?" asks Ms. Clam.

"No," says Mr. Fish.
"I'm going home," says a disappointed searcher, heading toward Rainbow Reef.

As Mr. Fish watches the small fish swim away, he has an idea.
"I think I know where my treasure is!" He darts off, and the others follow.

At the end of Rainbow Reef, in a hidden hollow, Mr. Fish finds what he is seeking: a school of shimmering yellow butterfly fish. "We've found the gold at the end of the rainbow!" Mr. Eight declares.

"We thought it would be fun to play hide-and-seek," say the mischievous golden fish as they swirl back into Mr. Fish's pot, completing his costume.

It is a happy parade home, now that Mr. Fish is reunited
with his little friends.

"What a lucky day!" says a smiling Mr. Fish.
"HAPPY ST. PATRICK'S DAY TO ONE AND ALL!"